D0355064

Karen's Mystery

**Look for these
and other books about Karen
in the
Baby-sitters Little Sister series:**

Little Sister

Karen's Mystery
Ann M. Martin

Illustrations by Susan Tang

A
LITTLE APPLE
PAPERBACK

SCHOLASTIC INC.
New York Toronto London Auckland Sydney

If you purchased this book without a cover you should be aware that this book is stolen property. It was reported as "unsold and destroyed" to the publisher and neither the author nor the publisher has received any payment for this "stripped book."

Activities by Nancy E. Krulik

No part of this publication may be reproduced in whole or in part, or stored in a retrieval system, or transmitted in any form or by any means, electronic, mechanical, photocopying, recording, or otherwise, without written permission of the publisher. For information regarding permission, write to Scholastic Inc., 730 Broadway, New York, NY 10003.

ISBN 0-590-44827-7

Copyright © 1991 by Ann M. Martin. All rights reserved. Published by Scholastic Inc. APPLE PAPERBACKS is a registered trademark of Scholastic Inc. BABY-SITTERS LITTLE SISTER is a trademark of Scholastic Inc.

12 11 10 9 8 7 6 5 4 3 2   4 5 6/9

Printed in the U.S.A.   40

First Scholastic printing, December 1991

For the Stoeckleins —
Alex, Rick,
Pierson, Hill, and Aristia

Karen's Mystery

December

I have a lot of favorite things. I have a favorite color (pink), and a favorite pet (my rat, Emily Junior), and a favorite teacher (Ms. Colman). I have a favorite month of the year, too. It is not the month of my birthday. It is not September when school starts. It is not June when summer vacation starts. It is . . . December.

December is a gigundoly wonderful month. Winter begins in December, and I love, love, love winter. Especially snow. I like snowmen and snowballs and snow

1

forts. I like snowflakes and snowstorms. Oh, and I like ice, too. Ice-skating and icicles.

Here are some other good things about December: winter vacation and, best of all, holidays. I celebrate Christmas. My friend Nancy celebrates Hanukkah. These are happy holidays. Also, we get presents.

Every year, I wait for December. It is too bad it's the last month of the year. I feel like I'm *always* waiting for December. December of second grade was especially hard to wait for. My mother and Seth (he's my stepfather) were going to go on a ski vacation for two whole weeks. So my brother, Andrew, and I would get to stay with our father. We would be at his house for Christmas! YEA!

I was packing up to go to Daddy's. I had to remember to bring a lot of important things. I had to remember the presents for my family at Daddy's. I had to remember my Hanukkah present for Nancy. And I had to remember my detective stuff.

Here is another one of my favorite things: solving mysteries. I just love mysteries and detectives. Maybe I will be a detective myself someday. Detectives get to poke around and look for clues. They find secret passages. They write notes in codes. They send messages to each other. They say things like, "The green bicycle crows at noon." And they understand what that means. Best of all, they get to spy.

I have been reading lots of detective books. I like the Bobbsey Twins. Bert and Nan and Freddie and Flossie solve gigundoly cool mysteries. Nan is my heroine. I like Encyclopedia Brown, too. Sometimes I can solve the cases before Encyclopedia does. And I like the Three Investigators.

My suitcase was getting full, but I still had to pack: my magnifying glass, my De-cod-R ring, *The Bobbsey Twins at the Seashore*, and my maze book. Mommy had bought the maze book for me. She said she hoped it would take my mind off Christmas.

(Sometimes I get just an eensy bit too excited about holidays.) The maze book was great. It was full of maps and secret passages and lost treasures. (I am very good at finding things.)

I tried to close my suitcase. I could do it if I sat on it. I had just snapped the lid shut when I remembered something. I remembered that I was not finished packing. I had to pack for someone else. I had to pack for Emily Junior. She would be going to Daddy's with me. I had to bring her cage and her food pellets and her water bottle and her toys. And I had to remember to bring Emily herself. (Well, she would be *in* the cage.)

I take extra-good care of Emily Junior. I feed her and give her fresh water. I play with her. I even plan to give her a birthday party next year. (Sometimes I forget and leave the top off her cage, but I am working on that.)

"Are you ready to go to Daddy's?" I

asked my rat. "Are you ready for Christmas? Are you ready for presents and vacation?"

It was too bad we had to wait until the next day for the fun to start.

2 + 2 = Karen

Guess what. I have told you about Emily Junior and about my friend Nancy. But I have not told you who *I* am!

I am Karen Brewer. But if I ever get to be an actress, I will use a stage name. My stage name will be Katerina Natalia. (Yesterday I decided it would be Francine von Fortunoff. Then I changed my mind.) I have a little brother named Andrew. Andrew is four, going on five. I am seven. There are a lot of things I have to teach Andrew.

Andrew and I have an awfully big family. This is because our mommy and daddy are divorced. They used to be married. Then my family was easy to describe: Mommy, Daddy, Andrew, me. But Mommy and Daddy decided that they did not want to live together anymore. They were through loving each other. So they got divorced. Mommy moved out of the big house we lived in. (It is the house where Daddy grew up.) Andrew and I moved with her. We moved to a little house. The little house and the big house are both in Stoneybrook, Connecticut.

After awhile, Mommy and Daddy got married again. But not to each other. Mommy married Seth. He lives with us at the little house. He brought along his dog, Midgie, and his cat, Rocky.

Daddy married Elizabeth. She is my stepmother. She lives at the big house with Daddy — and about a million other people. My big-house family is gigundo! Here is why. Elizabeth has four kids. They are my stepbrothers and stepsister. Charlie and Sam are old. They go to *high school*. David Michael is seven, like me. Actually, he is a few months older than I am. He never lets me forget it. My stepsister is Kristy. She is thirteen and she baby-sits. She is my favorite baby-sitter in the whole wide world. She is also one of my favorite people. I am glad she's my sister.

Emily Michelle lives at the big house, too. Emily is my adopted sister. She is two and a half years old. Daddy and Elizabeth adopted her from a country called Vietnam, which is very far away. (I named my rat after Emily.)

Also at the big house lives Nannie. Nannie is Elizabeth's mother, so that means she is my stepgrandmother. Nannie watches Emily while Daddy and Elizabeth are at work and everyone else is at school.

These are the big-house pets: Boo-Boo (Daddy's fat old cat); Shannon (David Michael's puppy); Crystal Light the Second (my goldfish); and Goldfishie (Andrew's guess what).

Since Andrew and I live at the big house every other weekend and on special vacations, it is a very busy place. I just love the big house.

Here is an interesting fact. Andrew and I have two of lots of things. We have two mommies, two daddies, two families, two houses, two cats, and two dogs. We have clothes and toys and books at each of our houses. I even have two best friends. Nancy Dawes is my little-house best friend. She lives next door to Mommy. My big-house best friend is Hannie Papadakis. She lives across the street from Daddy and one house down. Nancy and Hannie and I are all in Ms. Colman's second-grade class at Stoneybrook Academy. We call ourselves the Three Musketeers.

Since Andrew and I have two of so many things, I gave us special nicknames. I call us Andrew Two-Two and Karen Two-Two. (I got the name from a book Ms. Colman read to our class. It was called *Jacob Two-Two Meets the Hooded Fang*.) Sometimes being a two-two is confusing. But mostly it is fun. Like right now. I could not wait to go to the big house for two weeks. I was so, so excited!

The Big House

"We're here! Here we are! Hello, everybody!"

It was Saturday. It was time for our big-house adventure to begin.

That morning, Mommy had woken Andrew and me early. "Let's go, merry sunshine," she had said to me. "Get ready for Daddy's."

Andrew and I ate breakfast while Seth packed the car. He put the skis in a rack on the roof. (I was afraid they would fall off.)

When the car was packed, we drove to the big house. Andrew and I said good-bye to Mommy and Seth. (Andrew only cried a little.) Now we were standing in the doorway. Mommy and Seth were driving away. Daddy and Kristy and Nannie and *everyone* greeted us.

"Hi, Professor!" David Michael called to me. (He gave me that nickname because I wear glasses.) "Guess what. We are going to decorate the house today. The outside tree, too."

"Yea!" I cried. Decorating the house meant getting out our Christmas decorations — the manger, and the wooden angels for the mantelpiece and the bell to hang in the doorway and the music box that looks like Santa Claus. (We were not going to decorate the inside tree yet, though.)

"Before you get too excited," said Elizabeth, "please put your suitcases upstairs. And Karen, why don't you put Emily Junior and her cage in the playroom? *Then* we will begin decorating."

"Okay!" I ran upstairs. Andrew ran after me. I stuck my rat in the playroom. I closed the door so Boo-Boo could not get in.

When Andrew and I had put our things away, we ran downstairs again.

Daddy and Charlie and Kristy were outside. They were going to string lights on the fir tree in the front yard.

Everyone else was inside. They were opening boxes and looking at all the things we had not seen since the year before.

"There's the gold bell!" said David Michael.

"There's Santa!" exclaimed Andrew.

"And there's Rudolph, Rudolph, Rudolph!" I sang.

"Simmer down, Karen," said Elizabeth. (That meant I should calm down.)

"Sorry," I replied. I decided to help Nannie for awhile. Nannie was busy putting evergreen branches around the house. She put some on the mantel. Then Andrew stood on a chair and arranged an orchestra of tiny wooden angels in the branches.

They looked like they were playing music in a forest. Nannie put a branch over each picture frame in the living room. Sam hung ornaments from the branches. Finally Nannie tied several branches together with a red bow. She hung them on the front door.

"Oh, it's Christmastime, it's Christmastime!" I shouted.

"Indoor voice, Karen," said Nannie.

"Boo. Nannie, I am going outdoors," I replied. "Then I can use my loud voice."

I put on my jacket and my hat and my scarf and my mittens. I wanted to put on my boots, but I did not need them. There was no snow yet. I hoped snow would fall before Christmas.

When I joined Daddy and Charlie and Kristy, they were almost finished putting the lights on the tree. The tree was going to look gigundoly pretty. The lights were red and green. And the bulbs were big. (Last year, some of the bulbs disappeared. We do not know what happened to them. *I* think someone stole them. I hoped the

thief would leave our tree alone this year. I did not want any holes in our decorating job.)

Daddy turned on the lights then.

"Beautiful!" I exclaimed. Then I added, "Yea! Hurray! Hurray!"

Detective Karen

By lunchtime, the decorating was finished.

"Karen? Andrew?" said Elizabeth. "Have you unpacked your suitcases?"

My big-house family was in the kitchen. We were eating chicken 'n' stars soup. (The stars are really noodles.) Daddy was fixing a fruit salad.

"No," I answered. "We'll unpack after lunch. I might need some help with Emily Junior."

"What kind of help?" asked Daddy.

"I need to put her cage where she will be safe from Boo-Boo."

Sam snorted. "From Boo-Boo? Boo-Boo is too old to catch things. He probably wouldn't know what to do with a rat."

"I am not taking any chances," I replied. "Daddy, I think we should put the cage high up. But not so high up that I cannot reach it. Plus," I went on, "we have to fix Emily's water bottle. I took it out of the cage so it would not drip while we drove over here. I gave her a dish of water, but I bet she wants her bottle back now."

"Emily Junior is such a baby," whispered David Michael.

"I heard that!" I yelled. "And she is *not* a baby!"

"Before you two have a fight, let's go take care of Emily," Daddy said to me.

Daddy and I left the table. We went upstairs to the playroom.

Daddy looked around. "I think Emily Junior will be safe on this table," he said. "It isn't *too* high up."

"But Boo-Boo might jump on it," I told him. I felt worried.

"I don't think so," replied Daddy. "Emily will be safe."

Daddy fiddled around with the water bottle. I took Emily out of the cage. I let her run around on the floor.

"Careful, honey," said Daddy. "This is a big house. And it's new to Emily. She does not know her way around. Oh, and be sure to keep the top on the cage. You know how Nannie feels about rats.

"Now let me see. How does the bottle work?" Daddy continued. "Where are my glasses? I'll be right back, Karen."

When Daddy came back, he was frowning. "I can't find them," he said.

I jumped up. "I'm a good detective," I told him. "I will help you." I remembered to stick Emily in her cage and to put on the lid. Then I got out my magnifying glass and Decod-R ring. I walked all through the house.

"What are you doing?" David Michael

wanted to know. When I told him, he said. "I'm a good detective, too! We could be a team."

"Okay," I agreed. "Now let's think carefully. We should look in the places where Daddy has been today."

"Good idea," said David Michael.

First we looked in Daddy's bedroom, even though he had looked there himself. No glasses. We looked in the kitchen, where he had eaten breakfast and lunch. No glasses. We looked in the living room, where Daddy and Elizabeth had put the boxes of decorations. No glasses. We even looked in the attic, where the boxes of decorations had come from. No glasses.

"Maybe Emily Michelle wanted to play with them," I suggested. So we looked in Emily's room. No glasses.

"I know!" exclaimed David Michael. "Before you came over this morning, Daddy bought new lights for the tree. He needed his glasses to read the instructions on the box. Let's look in the den."

So we did. And I found Daddy's glasses lying on the floor. They must have fallen off a table. David Michael and I gave them to Daddy.

"You are wonderful detectives!" he said. "Thank you!"

The Mystery of the
Missing Cookies

I was very proud of David Michael and myself. We had solved the Mystery of Daddy's Glasses. And no grown-ups had helped us.

"Hey, David Michael. Let's solve some more mysteries," I said. "Want to?" (I had finished unpacking my suitcase.)

"Sure," he answered. "Do you know of any more mysteries?"

"No . . . but I'm sure one will come along."

I hoped this new game would be fun. I hoped it would do something else, too. I hoped it would take my mind off Christmas. I was definitely too excited. Elizabeth had told me to simmer down. Nannie had said to use my indoor voice. Daddy had said, "I cannot hear yellers, Karen." Andrew had said, "Too much noise!" And Kristy had said, "Could you talk a little louder, Karen? I don't think they can hear you in Denmark."

"Where is Denmark?" I had asked.

"Across the Atlantic Ocean."

I laughed. But I knew I needed to stop thinking about Christmas.

David Michael and I prowled all through the big house. We peered at things through the magnifying glass.

"Found any good mysteries yet?" asked Charlie.

"No," replied David Michael.

"But we will," I added.

All was quiet in the bedrooms and the

bathrooms and the living room. We crept into the kitchen. Nannie was there. She was baking cookies.

She looked cross.

"What's the matter?" I asked her.

Nannie frowned. "These cookies are for the bake sale," she said.

"I know. You told us at lunch," I answered. "You said not to eat any."

"But somebody *did* eat some. A whole handful is gone."

"Uh-oh," said David Michael.

I whispered to him, "Hey! It's the Mystery of the Missing Cookies!"

"Right," he agreed. "Let's get to work."

David Michael and I cased the joint. (That is what TV detectives say.) We searched for clues everywhere. We used my magnifying glass, but we did not need the Decod-R ring.

"Who are the suspects?" I asked.

"Everybody," replied David Michael. "Oh, except for us. And Nannie."

"And except for Kristy. She went to her

24

friend's house. And except for Charlie. He went to the store." (Charlie can drive. He even has a car of his own.) "Let's see," I went on. "That leaves Daddy and Elizabeth and Sam and Andrew and Emily Michelle. Let's look for footprints!"

My brother and I did not find any footprints in the kitchen.

"Okay. We better interview the suspects," I said.

We talked to Daddy and Elizabeth first. We asked them questions like, "When was the last time you were in the kitchen?" We decided they were not the thieves.

We looked for Sam, but we could not find him. So we interviewed Andrew next. As soon as we told him about the cookies, he screeched, "I did not take them! I understood what Nannie said!"

"Well, excuse me," I replied. "Come along, David Michael."

We found Emily in the playroom. She was trying on dress-up clothes.

And guess what. Her mouth was covered

26

with cookie crumbs! David Michael and I brought her into the kitchen. "I don't think she understood your warning," I told Nannie. (Nannie forgave Emily.)

Another case had been solved.

The Case of the
Mysterious Bird

"Jump, jump . . . Come on, JUMP!"

I am training Emily Junior to be a circus rat. Here is what she can do so far: run really fast.

I guess that does not sound like much. But just wait. I am sure that someday Emily will be able to turn a somersault, walk a tightrope, and fly through the air on a little rat trapeze. Right then, I was teaching her to jump through a hoop. Only I was teaching her in a box. The box was her playpen. Do you know what Sam had told me? He said that rats can get lost in walls and other places in big, old houses. So I was being careful. I did not want Emily to get lost.

"JUMP!" I commanded again.

Emily sniffed around her playpen.

"AUGHHHHH!"

I heard a scream. It came from downstairs. It sounded like Elizabeth.

"Yipes," I said. "Trouble."

I scooped up Emily Junior. I put her back in her cage. Then I ran downstairs. Halfway there, I remembered that I had not put the top on Emily's cage. Oh, well. Daddy had said the cage was in a safe place. I would remember to fix it later. Besides, a scream means a big problem.

"Elizabeth?" I called. I dashed into the kitchen.

Sam and Andrew and David Michael ran in also.

"What happened, Mom?" asked Sam.

Elizabeth tried to smile. "I'm sorry I screamed," she said. "But look." She pointed across the room to Boo-Boo's food dishes. In one was . . . a dead bird.

"Gross," said Sam.

"Does anyone know where that came from?" asked Elizabeth. "It is not a very funny trick. It is disgusting."

David Michael and I looked at each other. Another mystery!

"Don't worry," I told Elizabeth. "David Michael and I will crack the Case of the Mysterious Bird." Then I whispered to David Michael, "I bet this is one of Sam's tricks." My brother nodded.

"Never fear!" I called to Elizabeth.

David Michael and I ran back to the playroom. I remembered to put the lid on Emily's cage. Then my brother and I interviewed the people in my big-house family. We said, "How do you feel about birds?" and, "Have you played any practical jokes today?"

Sam had played several jokes. I was pretty sure he was the culprit. So David Michael and I looked for Elizabeth. We wanted to tell her the case was closed. She could rest easy. On our way to the TV room, we passed the back door to the house. Boo-Boo was waiting to be let in.

"Hey!" cried David Michael as he opened the door. "Boo-Boo caught a bird!"

"Oh, he couldn't have," I said. "Sam said Boo-Boo is too fat and lazy to catch anything. Remember? He said Boo-Boo never hunts."

"Well, he hunted for this bird. And he caught it," replied David Michael. "He must have caught the other bird, too. Boo-Boo was smart to put the bird in his food dish."

"I guess. Anyway, we have solved another mystery," I said. "We really are good detectives. Now we have solved *three* mysteries."

"We are crime-stoppers," added David Michael.

I nodded. Crime-stoppers. I liked the sound of that.

Hiding Places

I was feeling very cozy. My big-house family and I were curled up in the living room. Outside, the air was *freezing*. But Daddy and Kristy had built a fire in the fireplace. Now it was roaring.

Daddy was reading stories. He was reading them aloud. They were kids' stories, but my whole family was listening to them. Even Sam. First Daddy read *The Tailor of Gloucester*. It is by Beatrix Potter. I just love her books. They are gigundoly wonderful. Beatrix Potter has written lots of little books. Daddy was reading about the tailor because that's a Christmas story. I was hoping he would read *The Roly-Poly Pudding*, too, even though it is not about Christmas. Maybe he would also read *Squirrel Nutkin*. That story is so, so funny.

Elizabeth was sitting in an armchair. Emily Michelle was in her lap. I was in Kristy's lap. (I am almost too big for it.) David Michael was in Daddy's lap. While Daddy read, David Michael moved his lips. Andrew, Sam, and Charlie were lying on the floor, near the fireplace. And Nannie was next to Kristy and me. She was knitting a sweater for Andrew.

See why I felt cozy? The living room was warm. And it was quiet, except for the sound of Daddy reading and Nannie's needles clicking.

The Tailor of Gloucester is about a poor, old tailor who lived in a town in the country of England long ago. The tailor had a cat named Simpkin. And Simpkin liked mice. (So do I.) The mice in Gloucester ran all

33

through the town — without ever going out-of-doors. They ran from house to house in little passages behind walls. They knew lots of hiding places.

When Daddy finished reading the story, I said, "Now could you please, please, puh-*lease* read *The Roly-Poly Pudding*?"

So Daddy did. That is a story about these two rats who scurry around behind the walls of a country house and catch a naughty kitten who is exploring the inside of the chimney.

"Well, that's interesting," said Sam, as Daddy put the book down.

"What is?" I asked.

"All those rats getting lost behind walls in old houses. Maybe you better remember that the next time you take Emily Junior out of her cage. This is a big, old house."

"Oh, Sam," I said. "Those were *mice* in *The Tailor of Gloucester*. And they did not really get lost. Simpkin *trapped* them under teacups. And the rats in *The Roly-Poly Pud-*

ding did not get lost, either. They were the ones who caught the kitten."

"I am just saying," went on Sam, "that a lot of *rodents* were running around behind the walls in houses."

"Yeah, be careful with Emily Junior," said Andrew.

"She does not know this house very well," added David Michael. "She could fall into a heating vent or get stuck in the attic."

"Or go down the drain," said Sam. (Charlie punched him.)

"Or run out into the hall and sail right between the railings of the banister and fall all the way to the first floor," said David Michael. "Splat."

"Okay, okay. Enough," said Daddy.

"Anyway, Emily Junior is not going to get lost because she is not going to get loose," I said firmly.

"I hope not," said Elizabeth and Nannie.

Me, too, I thought. I felt a teensy bit worried.

The Three Investigators

Emily Junior had not gotten loose, of course. I checked on her as soon as Daddy finished reading. There she was, safe in her cage. She was waking up from a nap. She was getting ready to play.

I made sure the lid was on the cage. Then I said to my rat, "Good night, sleep tight, don't let the bedbugs bite."

The next day was Sunday. Hannie and Nancy came over to play.

"Yea!" I cried. "The Three Musketeers,

together again!" (We had been together on Friday, but that seemed like ages ago.)

My friends and I raced to my bedroom.

"Last one there is a rotten egg!" shouted Hannie. Hannie ended up as the rotten egg. She did not care.

"What should we do today?" asked Nancy. She and Hannie and I had flopped onto my bed. (I was holding my nose since Hannie was a rotten egg.)

"I doe! Let's solve bysteries," I said.

"Stop holding your nose, Karen," ordered Hannie. "I cannot understand you."

"I said we should solve mysteries. David Michael and I were detectives yesterday and we solved *three* mysteries." I told my friends about tracking down Daddy's glasses and fingering Emily Michelle and Boo-Boo. (That means we found the criminals.)

"Wow!" cried Nancy. "Maybe we could start a detective agency." (Nancy and

Hannie had been reading mysteries, too. They like them almost as much as I do.)

"Yeah," I agreed. "And since we are the Three Musketeers, we will call ourselves the Three Investigators. Just like the kids in those books."

"Yeah!" cried Nancy.

"Yeah!" cried Hannie.

"If we are going to have an agency," said Nancy, thinking hard, "and a name, then we should hang a sign on the door."

"Okay," I replied. I found a large piece of paper. Hannie got out my Magic Markers. We got right to work. When we were finished, this is how our sign looked:

THE THREE INVESTAGATORS
SUPER-DETECTIVES
WE SOLVE MYSTERIES
NO CASE TOO TOUGH

Then Nancy and I stuck the sign on my door. We used Scotch tape, but not too

much. Daddy says it can take paint off, and I did not want to do anything bad to my door. Especially not right before Christmas.

"What should we do first?" asked Hannie.

The sign was up, and we were sitting in my room. I guess we were waiting for a mystery to begin.

"Hmm, I know," I said. "I will be the head detective, and I will teach you guys how to solve crimes. I will show you how to use my magnifying glass and Decod-R ring. Then I will show you how to dust for fingerprints. Good detectives learn lots of things from fingerprints. That is because they are like snowflakes. No two are the same. You can make fingerprints show up by sprinkling powder over them. Then you just have to find out who they belong to. Also, you should look at footprints. If you can tell whose shoes they came from, then you might be able to catch a thief. Oh, and maybe we should learn how to make disappearing ink. And — "

"Karen?" Nancy interrupted me. "How are people going to know about our agency?"

Uh-oh. Good question.

9

No Case Too Tough

"We need to let everyone know about the Three Investigators, Super-Detectives," said Nancy. "But only the people in your family will see our sign, Karen."

"Right. We better advertise," I replied. "Okay, let's make fliers. We can give them to our friends."

"And to our neighbors and families," added Hannie.

I found some construction paper. Then Hannie and Nancy and I sat at the table in my room. We copied the words from our sign onto the papers.

We worked very hard.

When a voice said, "Hey! What are you doing?" I jumped a mile.

"David Michael!" I exclaimed. "Don't sneak up on us."

"I didn't," he said. "I was very noisy. You just did not hear me." David Michael pointed to the sign. "What does that mean?" he asked.

"We have started a detective agency," said Hannie proudly.

"And it was *my* idea," added Nancy.

David Michael's mouth dropped open. "What about *me*?" he cried. "It was *my* idea to solve mysteries. I had the idea yesterday."

"We-ell . . ." I said. "But Nancy thought up the agency."

"So let me join," said my brother. "Let me be a detective in your agency."

"But you can't be. You are not a Three

Musketeer," I told him. "This detective agency is for the Three Musketeers. Besides, if you joined, we would have to change our sign and the fliers. They would have to say, 'The *Four* Investigators.' I do not want to change everything."

"That is not fair!" cried David Michael.

"Is too," I shouted.

"Is not."

"Is too."

"Not."

"Too."

"All ri-ight," said David Michael. "See if I care. But I am warning you, Karen. I will never solve another mystery with you again."

"Fine. I do not need your help."

"Do too," said David Michael.

"Not."

"Too. And anyway, your — "

"I know, I know. My epidermis is showing," I said. My brothers are always trying to get me with that stupid skin joke.

David Michael stomped down the hall. "I hope you get a stocking full of coal on Christmas morning!" he yelled.

"I hope you get two," I yelled back. "One for each foot." I do not like to joke about Christmas, but David Michael had made me mad. He had taken some of the fun out of the Three Investigators.

When we had made a stack of fliers, Hannie and Nancy and I took them outdoors. We gave them to our friends and neighbors.

"No case too tough," we told everyone.

"How much do you charge?" asked Linny Papadakis. (He is Hannie's older brother.)

I glanced at my friends. They shrugged. I said, "I don't know. I guess we are free. We work really hard, though."

"No case too tough," added Nancy.

But no one needed a mystery solved.

The Mysterious
Disappearing Present

The Three Investigators handed out the fliers. Then we went back to my room. "We will make more," I said. "Let's keep working."

We sat at the table. But after a few minutes, Nancy said, "I have to go home soon. Mommy is coming for me."

"Now?" I replied. "It is still early."

"I know. But tonight is the beginning of Hanukkah. I have to be home before sundown. Then Mommy and Daddy and I will light the first candle on the menorah. And we will each get a present," added Nancy.

I jumped up. "Hey! I just thought of something," I exclaimed. "I have a Hanukkah present for you. You should take it home with you."

"Thanks," said Nancy. She was smiling.

I ran to the drawer where I had hidden my presents. I opened the drawer.

It was empty!

I gasped.

"What's wrong?" asked Hannie.

"I hid all my presents right here," I said. "And now they are gone."

"A mystery!" cried Nancy.

"Yeah, the first case for the Three Investigators," I added.

"Karen, did anyone see you hide the presents in the drawer?" asked Hannie.

I thought hard. Then I cried. "Yes! Andrew did. I bet he took them."

"What a sneak," said Nancy.

"But wait. Why would he want the present I got for Elizabeth?"

"What did you get her?" asked Hannie.

"A carrot peeler."

Hannie raised her eyebrows. "Why?"

I shrugged. "She said she did not have one."

My friends and I thought some more. Soon Nancy said, "I have an idea. Karen, try to remember everything you did with the presents today."

"Okay." I frowned. "Let me see. When I got up this morning, I checked on them right away. I opened the drawer and I counted them. All there. Then, after breakfast, I decided to — Oh! That's it! I decided to wrap them. Now I remember. So I carried the presents downstairs to the den. And I said, 'Everybody, keep out! No peeking! Privacy, please.' "

"Then you wrapped the presents?" asked Nancy.

I nodded.

"And then I — I left them in the living room so I can put them under the tree after we decorate it."

"That's where Nancy's present must be then," said Hannie. "In the living room."

"No. I do not think so. See, I only put *family* presents there."

"Where did you put the other presents?"

"There were no others," I replied. "Except for Nancy's." (I had not bought Hannie's present yet.)

"Come on, you guys," said Hannie. "Karen, I bet your forgot and put Nancy's present in the living room with the others. Let's look."

So we did. And there was the present for Nancy!

"Open it before your mom comes," I said.

Nancy tore the paper off the package. "Oh, thank you!" she exclaimed. "This is cool, Karen. An activity book about mysteries and detectives. Mazes, riddles, puzzles . . . ooh, crossword puzzles! This is great."

"Happy Hanukkah, Nancy," I said. Then I heard Nancy's mom honking the car horn. "See you tomorrow," I added. "Maybe the Three Investigators will find another mystery."

"She's Gone!"

"Well, good night, Moosie. Good night, Tickly," I said. I was ready to climb into bed. I planned to read for awhile. Supper was over. The weekend was over. And I was tired. Starting a detective agency is very hard work. So is being the head detective.

I jumped up. "Uh-oh. Guess what, Moosie. I almost forgot to say good night to Emily Junior," I said. I ran into the playroom. Right away, I saw that I had left the top off Emily's cage. (Again.) "It's a good thing I came in here, Emily. I would not want you to — Yikes!"

I could not see Emily in the cage.

I leaned over. I stared all around.

Then, "Aughhh!" I screamed. "She's gone!"

I could hear footsteps. Kristy ran into the playroom. Daddy was right behind her. And Nannie and Charlie were behind them.

"What's the matter?" cried Kristy. "Are you all right?"

I shook my head. "No. Emily Junior is gone! I came in to tell her good night and her cage was empty."

"Oh, Karen," whispered Nannie.

Daddy was giving me a Look.

But Kristy said, "Maybe if you study her cage, you can find a clue to what happened to her, Karen. Don't disturb anything. Just use your eyes."

I examined the cage. The top was lying

on the floor where I had left it. But everything *in* the cage looked fine. Nothing was missing. Nothing was messed up.

"No sign of a struggle," I announced.

"Then Emily Junior must have escaped," said Charlie.

"We have to find her!" I cried. "Oh, no. This is an awful mystery."

"I think I will go downstairs," said Nannie. She tippety-toed out of the playroom. She looked as if she were afraid she would step on something icky.

I began to cry. "I'm sorry, Daddy," I said. "I did not mean to let Emily escape. I do not even remember leaving the top off her cage. Hey! Maybe I *didn't* leave off the top. Maybe Emily was kidnapped."

"Oh, Karen," said Charlie. "You were the one who said there was no sign of a struggle. Besides, you always forget to put the top on the cage."

Kristy put her arm around me. Daddy gave me a kiss. "You better start looking," said Daddy. "Maybe we can find Emily Junior before you go to bed."

Emily Michelle was already asleep, but everyone else said they would help me search. Even David Michael said so. Even *Nannie*.

"Thank you," I replied. "Let's begin the search here in the playroom." Then I thought of something horrible. "Oh, no!" I shrieked. "What if Boo-Boo got Emily Junior? We did not think he could catch birds, but he caught two. Maybe he caught Emily, also."

"I doubt it," said Sam. "I am sure Emily is just running around the house. I hope she finds the kitchen, though. It would be awful if she starved."

"Or got stepped on," said Andrew. "What if someone was just walking along and then the person stepped on Emily and tripped and fell down the stairs and crash-landed at the bottom and — "

"Enough, Andrew," said Daddy.

David Michael leaned over to me. You

know what he whispered in my ear? He whispered, "Hey, Karen, I do not want to scare you, but I read that rats can squeeze down to an inch or two and fit into teeny-tiny spaces. Even fat rats can do that. So we better search carefully. Emily Junior could be anywhere."

Upstairs and Downstairs

We started the hunt for Emily in the playroom. My big-house family spread out. We looked under chairs and couches. We looked behind bookcases. Andrew looked in the toy chest. "If I were a rat, this is where I would hide," he said. "Then I would stay up all night and play."

"Is Emily Junior a good climber?" Charlie asked me.

"Oh, she is very good," I answered. "I am training her for the rat circus."

"Then we better look up high, too. Not

just down low." Charlie began to poke through the books on the shelves.

"We better look everywhere," I added. David Michael had said that rats can squeeze down to eensy sizes. So Emily Junior could be —

Under the rug! Yipes! What if she had crawled under the rug and we were stepping all over her? There were no lumps in the rug, but I lifted a corner and peered underneath. No Emily. Even so, I called out, "Everybody, watch where you step!"

Then I looked for Emily under a cowboy hat. I looked between the cushions on the couch. I peered inside the dollhouse. I looked in a box of crayons.

"Stop fooling around, Karen," said Sam.

"I am not fooling around. I am being — I am being — "

"Thorough," supplied Elizabeth. "Karen is being thorough."

"Thank you," I said.

Daddy looked at his watch. "It is getting late," he announced. "We have a whole house to search. I think we should spread out."

Nannie and Elizabeth and David Michael and Charlie went downstairs. Daddy and Andrew and Sam and Kristy and I stayed upstairs. We decided we should each search different rooms.

"I will check all the bathrooms," I announced.

First I went into the bathroom I share with Andrew and David Michael and Emily Michelle. "Goodness," I said. "I will have to check a lot of places in here. If Emily Junior can shrink, she could be inside that plastic boat. She could have gone down the drain in the sink. Or in the bathtub." I leaned into the bathtub. I yelled down the drain, "Hey, Emily, are you in there? You come out right now!"

No Emily.

I looked under the bathroom rug. I looked in a pile of towels. I looked in the toilet.

No Emily.

60

I decided that the search for Emily was like a treasure hunt. Except there were no clues to follow. And the treasure was Emily.

"Hey, everybody! We're on a treasure hunt!" I yelled.

"Indoor voice, please, Karen," said Daddy. "Emily Michelle is asleep."

"Sorry," I replied. "Daddy, can you please come here?"

Daddy joined me in the bathroom.

"What if Emily Junior slid down the laundry chute?" I asked.

"The door to the chute is closed, honey," said Daddy. "You do not need to worry about that."

I checked the basement anyway.

No Emily.

My big-house family and I searched for more than an hour. We searched *every-where*. No Emily.

"This treasure hunt is not fun," I said.

The Vanishing Lights

I had been sure we would find Emily Junior before I went to bed that night.

But we did not. No Emily.

When I woke up on Monday morning — no Emily.

I went to the playroom. I stared sadly into Emily's cage.

"Empty," I said. A tear rolled down my cheek.

At school that day, I was very sad. I hardly talked at all. I did not raise my hand.

For Show and Share, Natalie Springer brought in the mouse her brother had bought at the pet store.

"His name is Delroy," said Natalie. "He is a very nice pet."

I burst into tears. "Emily Junior was a nice pet, too," I wailed. "And now she is gone. She is missing." I blew my nose. "She is at large," I added.

When I came home after school, I yelled, "Hey, Nannie? Any sign of Emily?"

Nannie shook her head. "Sorry," she said. "Not a trace." (I noticed that Nannie was wearing big, tall boots. And blue jeans.) "I certainly hope we find her soon," Nannie added.

"Me, too," I said, trying not to cry.

Later that afternoon I heard Kristy shout, "Oh, no!"

I ran downstairs. "Did you find Emily?" I asked.

"Nope. But the Bulb Thief has struck

again. Look." Kristy was standing at the front door. She pointed outside. She had just turned on the Christmas tree lights. A bunch of bulbs were missing.

"Maybe they are loose," I said. "Or maybe they burned out." I put on my jacket. I went outdoors. The bulbs really were missing! Wow. Another mystery to solve. I ran back to Kristy. "The bulbs have been stolen," I told her. "And I think the Bulb Thief is also a Rat Thief. I bet the same person who stole the light bulbs stole Emily Junior."

"Maybe," said Kristy.

I dashed to the telephone. I called Hannie. I told her about the thief. Then I said, "I have a plan. The thief strikes after dark. So tomorrow evening, let's stake out the tree. We will find a good hiding place. Then we will spy. We will watch the tree until the thief comes to rob the bulbs again."

Hannie said she would come over at five o'clock. Then I called Nancy. She was interested in the thief, but she would not be able to come to the stakeout. The next night would be the third night of Hanukkah. I hoped Hannie and I could catch the thief ourselves.

Caught!

On Tuesday morning, Emily's cage was still empty.

On Tuesday afternoon, it was still empty.

"Oh, well," I said to Nannie. "Who cares? In a couple of hours we will catch the thief. Then I will have Emily back, and you will not have to wear those boots all day. I hope the thief will give back our light bulbs, too."

At a quarter to five, I began to get ready for the stakeout. I found a flashlight. I found Daddy's Polaroid camera. I found a blanket to help keep Hannie and me warm. I tried to think what TV detectives bring on stakeouts. I remembered two important things. "Nannie?" I said. "Could I please have a box of doughnuts and a Thermos of coffee?"

Nannie looked quite surprised, but all she said was, "Not before dinner, honey."

Guess what? Kristy came on the stakeout with Hannie and me. "You might need some help," she said. "Besides, I want to catch the thief, too."

Kristy and Hannie and I hid in the garage. We turned off the light. Then we stood near the window. (We had opened the window so we could see better.) The fir tree was just outside the window.

"When the thief comes," I whispered, "we will snap his picture. Then we can prove who he is. And then we can get back Emily and the bulbs."

Hannie and my sister and I waited and waited. We huddled under the blanket. We were very quiet. We were patient, too. I bet

we stood in the cold garage for a week or so. That is how I felt. My toes grew numb.

Finally Hannie whispered, "Karen?"

"*SHHH!*" I hissed. "I heard something."

We peered through the window. From out of the darkness tiptoed a figure. Someone else was behind him (or her). I held my breath. The figures began to unscrew our Christmas bulbs!

Kristy nudged me in the side.

Silently I lifted the camera.

Click! Flash!

"Caught you!" I cried as the flash went off.

The thieves started to run away, but Kristy said, "It's a Polaroid camera, so you might as well stay here. In a few seconds we will know who you are."

Hannie turned on the light in the garage. Kristy ran into the yard. I watched the picture develop. "Hey, the thieves are — "

"PJ and Randall," Kristy said. She was leading them into our spy headquarters. I knew PJ and Randall. They are big kids.

They live over on Bertrand Drive. They go to my school. They are always in trouble. They are sister and brother. (PJ is the sister. Her real name is Polly Jean.)

At that moment, Daddy came home from work. He drove to the garage. He pulled up just in time to see PJ and Randall empty the pockets of their jackets. Their pockets were full of bulbs from Christmas trees!

"We caught the Bulb Thieves!" I announced. "Here is proof." I showed Daddy the Polaroid picture.

"We caught them red-handed," added Hannie.

"You certainly did," replied Daddy. He turned to PJ and Randall.

But before Daddy could say anything, I asked them the most important question of all: "Where is my rat?"

"Huh?" said PJ and Randall.

The Bulb Thieves had not stolen Emily Junior.

On the Loose

Daddy asked Randall and PJ to come inside with us.

"Do we *have* to?" they whined. But they came in anyway.

Then Daddy asked Randall and PJ to apologize for stealing, and for making everyone's decorations look so stinky.

"Sorry," mumbled Randall and PJ.

After that, Daddy called their parents.

"Hello, Mr. Rivers?" he said. "This is Watson Brewer. Your children, PJ and Randall, were caught removing bulbs from our outdoor Christmas tree. I would appreciate your coming over here and taking them home."

Mr. and Mrs. Rivers drove right over. Boy, were they mad! Especially after they looked at the picture I had snapped.

"You are grounded forever!" they said to Randall and PJ. (I do not think they meant that.)

The Riverses went home. Hannie went home.

Daddy said, "Karen, you are a wonderful detective."

"You solved the Mystery of the Vanishing Lights very quickly," added Kristy.

"Thank you," I replied. But I did not feel happy. Emily was still missing. I had not solved my most important mystery.

After school the next day, the Three Investigators were back in business. Hannie and Nancy came over. First, we ate a snack with Kristy and Sam. We sat at the table in the kitchen. We ate slices of apple and pieces of cheese.

When Sam finished, he stood up. "Well, I have homework," he said.

"Me, too," said Kristy.

"Just a minute," said Nannie. "Please clean up the kitchen."

Sam and Kristy and Nancy and Hannie and I wiped off the table. We threw away our napkins. We put the leftover cheese in the refrigerator.

"Thank you," said Nannie.

My friends and I moved to the den. A few minutes later we heard Nannie cry, "*Now* who is making messes?"

"Come on, you guys," I said to Hannie and Nancy. "Something is up." We raced into the kitchen. "What's wrong?" I asked Nannie.

Nannie pointed to the table. It was covered with crumbs!

"It wasn't us," said Nancy. "We are innocent. Besides, we were not eating crumby food."

"This is a mystery," I said solemnly. "Everybody think."

"Maybe Emily Michelle did it," said Hannie. "She turned out to be the Cookie Thief."

"Emily is taking a nap," replied Nannie.

"Maybe," I began slowly, "somebody was stealing food for Emily *Junior*. The thief has to feed her."

Nancy shook her head. "A thief would not leave such a mess. I bet Emily Junior took the food herself."

"Oh, dear," whispered Nannie. She looked at her feet. Luckily, she was still wearing her clompy boots and her blue jeans.

"Uh-oh," I said. "If Emily is on the loose, what about Boo-Boo? Emily might be Boo-Boo's next meal."

"Oh, dear," said Nannie again.

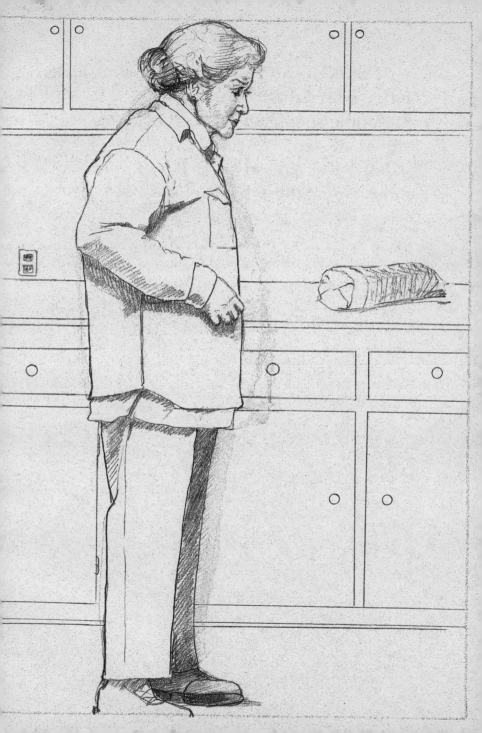

"Nannie? Do you think Boo-Boo looks fatter than usual?" I asked.

Nannie shook her head. "Of course not," she answered.

But I was not so sure. Boo-Boo is enormous no matter what.

The Booby Trap

On Wednesday night, we had a winter surprise. A blizzard! The wind blew and the snow fell. On Thursday we had a snow day. No school. When I woke up, snow covered everything! We would have snow for Christmas. By the afternoon, the snowplows had been grinding around Stoneybrook. Hannie came to my house to play. Mrs. Dawes was able to drive Nancy over.

As soon as the Three Investigators had gathered in my room, I said, "I have a plan. I know how we can catch the Rat Thief."

"You do?" said Hannie.

"Yup. This is what I think. If PJ and Randall could steal our bulbs, then someone could steal Emily Junior. We set up a trap and we caught PJ and Randall. So we will set up another trap to catch the Rat Thief. We will set up a booby trap."

"Way cool!" exclaimed Hannie.

"What kind of booby trap?" asked Nancy.

"A food booby trap," I replied. "See, I was thinking about the crumbs Nannie found on the kitchen table. Maybe they *were* left by the Rat Thief. Maybe he was stealing food for Emily and he heard Nannie coming, so he left in a hurry. He did not have time to clean up his mess."

"How do you know the thief is a 'he'?" asked Hannie.

I paused. "Well, I don't," I said. "The thief could be a 'she.' But it is easier to say 'he' than to say 'he or she' all the time. Anyway, this is my idea. The thief cannot keep raiding the kitchen. That is too risky.

He might get caught. So I bet the thief will try to steal Emily's rat pellets for her. They are in the playroom. All we have to do is booby-trap that bag of pellets and then spy on the playroom."

"Good idea," said Nancy.

We tied a string to the food bag. We fixed it so that if someone tried to open the bag it would fall over. Pellets would scatter everywhere! They would make a big mess and maybe some noise, too.

"Now what?" asked Hannie.

"Now we spy," I answered.

My friends and I tiptoed behind the couch. We were very quiet. We took turns peeping over the top of the couch. When we did that, we had a good view of Emily Junior's bag of food pellets. We waited and spied and waited and spied.

"This is boring," said Hannie finally.

"I will have to go home soon," said Nancy.

"My bottom is sore," I added.

Hannie and Nancy and I began to giggle.

I stood up and rubbed my bottom. Then I said. "I better check our booby trap. I want to make sure it still works."

It worked, all right. I know because I tripped over the string and knocked the bag to the floor. *Crash!* Then *whoosh* — pellets everywhere.

My friends helped me to clean up the mess. While we worked, I said. "You know, I sort of forgot that Emily could be running around behind the walls. I think we should look for a place where she went into the wall. We should look for her rat hole."

"Good idea," said Nancy.

At last the food pellets were back in the bag.

"Let the search begin," I said.

The Rat Hole

The Three Investigators investigated the playroom first.

"What are we looking for?" asked Nancy.

"Yeah," said Hannie. "A rat hole like in the cartoons? A tunnel into the wall? With a sign hanging out front that says, 'Attention, all cats. Rat in here'? And maybe a piece of cheese by the hole?"

"Maybe we should follow Boo-Boo," teased Nancy. "I bet *he* knows where Emily is. He could show us to the rat hole."

"Gimme a break," I said. But I laughed.

I liked my friends' jokes. "No. We are just looking for any little crack or hole or opening that Emily could have slipped through to get inside the wall."

We stooped to our hands and knees. We crawled around on the floor.

Hannie found an old chewed-up piece of gum. It was stuck to the wall behind a chair.

"I bet David Michael did that," I said.

Nancy found the missing red piece from our checkers game.

"Thank you!" I exclaimed.

I found a dime.

"Finders, keepers!" I cried. I stuffed the dime into my pocket.

After awhile, Nancy said, "We have looked everywhere in here." This was true. We had crawled around the entire room.

"I did not see even a little crack," added Hannie.

"Move into the hallway, troops," I ordered.

We crawled into the hall. We ran our hands along the baseboard. We had almost reached Andrew's room when Nancy cried, "Hey!"

"What is it?" asked Hannie and I.

"Look over here," replied Nancy.

We crawled next to Nancy. We could see little grayish-white things lying on the floor.

"They look like tiny pieces of chewed-up paper towels," I said. "Emily Junior likes to chew up paper towels. And *those* things look like crumbs!"

"The crumbs lead over here," said Hannie. "They make a trail."

We followed the trail along the hallway. The trail came to an end . . . by a crack in the baseboard! "Get a flashlight!" I shrieked.

Nancy found my flashlight. We peered inside the crack.

"I see more crumbs," said Hannie.

"This is it!" I cried. "The rat hole! Emily Junior must be in there!"

Found!

"**W**e have to get Emily out!" I exclaimed. I leaned over to the crack. I cupped my hands around my mouth. "Hey, Emily Junior!" I yelled. "Come on out of there!"

"Karen," said Nancy, "if I were a rat, all that yelling would scare me."

"Yeah," agreed Hannie. "We should do nice things to try to get Emily out."

"We'll *lure* her out," I said.

"What kinds of things does Emily especially like?" asked Nancy.

I thought. "Food," I answered. "But I do

not think Emily is hungry. I think she has been eating. She left an awful lot of crumbs. . . . She likes music," I added.

"Put her favorite song on the tape deck," said Hannie.

I went back to the playroom. I found the cassette player. I began to play the music from *Charlotte's Web*. (Emily likes the song sung by Templeton the rat.) I blasted the music into the crack.

No Emily.

"Let's try being really calm," suggested Nancy. She tapped her fingers on the wall. Then she called softly, "Emily, Emily, come on ou-out. Please come out, Emily Junior. Emily, your friends are waiting for you."

No Emily.

"I know!" I said suddenly. I ran into the playroom and found one of Emily's toys. A ball with a bell inside. I brought the toy to the rat hole. I shook it, making the bell jingle. "Emileeeee," I called. "I have a toy for you."

No Emily.

I was waiting for her to poke her nose and whiskers through the crack. But nothing happened.

Finally I lay on the floor. I put my fingers as far inside the wall as I could. I wiggled them around. "Come on, Emileeeee," I called.

From behind me I could hear laughter. I yanked my hand out of the wall and whirled around. There stood David Michael.

"What is so funny?" I asked.

"Yeah, what is so funny?" said Nancy and Hannie.

"You are," replied David Michael. "You guys are crawling all over the floor, trying to get a fat rat out of a teeny, tiny hole. Emily Junior is not in there — "

I narrowed my eyes. Slowly I got to my feet. "How do you know?" I asked.

"Because she is in my room," said David Michael smugly.

"You took her?" I yelped. "*You took* Emily Junior?"

A fight was brewing.

"Gotta go," said my friends. They went downstairs.

David Michael and I faced each other in the hall. My fists were clenched.

"What is she doing in your room?" I asked, "*Did* you take her?"

My brother nodded.

"But why?"

"I was mad at you."

"Because I would not let you be in the detective agency?" I said.

David Michael nodded his head again. "Yup."

"Then I am telling!" I shouted. "As soon as I check on my rat." I dashed into David Michael's bedroom.

Tattletale

"Where is Emily Junior?" I demanded.

"She's in the closet," said David Michael.

"In the closet?" I shrieked. "You locked my rat in a dark *closet*?"

"I did not *lock* her in," David Michael replied crossly. "She is in there in a special box. I fixed it up myself. Just for Emily Junior. And I left the light on. She is not in the dark."

I peeped in the closet. Sure enough, the light was on. And there was Emily curled up in a box. She was sound asleep. She looked just fine.

"Okay, *now* I am telling!" I exclaimed.

I shut the door to the closet. I marched downstairs. (Hannie and Nancy were not there. They had gone home.) But Kristy was there. And Nannie. And Daddy and Elizabeth. They were talking in the living room.

"Well, I found Emily Junior," I announced. I stood in the middle of the living room with my hands on my hips.

"You did?" cried Kristy.

"Yes," I answered. "And guess where." Before anyone could guess, I said, "I found her in David Michael's closet."

"Is she okay?" asked Elizabeth.

David Michael had joined us in the living room.

I glanced at him. He looked embarrassed. Even so, I said, "I don't know. How would you feel if someone had locked you in a closet for four days?"

"I already told you — I did not lock her in!" shouted David Michael.

"What is going on, you two?" asked Daddy.

"David Michael stole my rat!" I cried.

Daddy, Elizabeth, Nannie, and Kristy turned to David Michael.

"Is that true?" asked Elizabeth.

David Michael hung his head. "I guess."

"But why? You knew Karen was worried about Emily Junior. We all were." Elizabeth was frowning.

"Well, I was angry at Karen." David Michael told them about the Three Investigators, and how I would not let him be the fourth investigator.

"That was not very nice, Karen," said Daddy.

"Plus, Karen is a tattletale," said David Michael.

Daddy sighed. "Let's go take a look at Emily," he said.

Everyone followed David Michael upstairs and into his room. David Michael showed off the box he had kept my rat in. "See? I put her food here and her water here. And every day I gave her some exercise. I took good care of her. I even bought her a Christmas present."

"Did you leave the crumbs in the kitchen?" asked Nannie.

David Michael nodded. "I was getting a treat for Emily Junior. I had been feeding her the pellets, but I thought she might like some cake."

"What about the rat hole?" I asked.

My brother laughed. "That is just a crack in the wall. But I put the crumbs and stuff there to make you *think* it was a rat hole. And you did!"

"Meanie-mo!" I cried. I raised my fist in the air. Daddy caught my arm. "I know, I know," I said. "No fighting. Use words."

"But use them when you have calmed down," added Daddy. "Karen, David Michael, I am not pleased with what either of you did. So no allowance for a week. That goes for both of you."

"Boo," I said. I picked up Emily Junior and cuddled her. "At least you are safe," I said. "I promise I will never let you get kidnapped again."

Case Closed

My big mystery was over. The case was closed. Emily Junior was in her cage where she belonged. (And the lid was on.)

That evening I sat by myself in the living room. I looked at the mistletoe Daddy had hung over the doorway. I looked at the wooden angels and the golden bell and the musical Santa Claus. Then I stood by the window. I looked outside at the lighted trees on our street. And at our own tree with its red and green bulbs. Each bulb was glowing. Since I had caught PJ and Randall, no more bulbs had disappeared.

I thought about the things that had happened since Andrew and I had arrived at the big house. I thought of the mysteries David Michael and I had solved. The Mystery of Daddy's Glasses, the Mystery of the Missing Cookies, the Case of the Mysterious Bird. I remembered finding the Mysterious Disappearing Present with Hannie and Nancy. And, of course, catching the Bulb Thieves. Solving mysteries with David Michael had been fun. So had solving mysteries with Nancy and Hannie.

Then I remembered something else. I remembered the time Hannie was planning to get married to her friend, Scott Hsu. (Just pretend married.) First, Hannie asked me to be her bridesmaid. Then she told me I could not be her bridesmaid. I had felt awful. I had cried. Finally she had told me I could be her bridesmaid after all. Then I felt okay again.

I turned away from the window. I left the

living room and went upstairs to find David Michael. He was lying on his bed, doing nothing. When I came in, he looked over at me.

"Thanks to you," he said, "I cannot get the pin I was going to buy Nannie for Christmas. I needed *all* of my allowance for that."

"Sorry," I said. Then I added, "Well, thanks to *you*, I cannot buy the musical socks I wanted to get Hannie for Christmas."

David Michael rolled over. He turned his back to me. "Big deal," he muttered.

"David Michael?"

"What?"

"I'm sorry we would not let you in the detective agency," I said.

"You are?"

"Yeah. I just did not want to change the name of our agency. That was pretty silly. You are a very good detective."

"Thanks. I'm sorry I took Emily Junior and made you worry," said David Michael.

"Really?"

"Yeah. That was mean. I would not like it if someone took Shannon." David Michael rolled over again. Now he was facing me. I sat next to him.

"Did you really buy a Christmas present for Emily?" I asked.

"Yup. I'll show you what I got." David Michael pulled out a drawer in his desk. He took out a little box. "Look inside," he said.

I opened the box. I saw an eensy Christmas tree, decorated and everything.

"It is supposed to go in a dollhouse," said my brother. "But I thought you could put it in Emily's cage. She should have a Christmas tree."

"Oh, thank you!" I exclaimed. "Emily will love it."

"Can I give it to her?" asked David Michael.

"Sure," I replied. "And you know what else? You can be in the detective agency if

you want. 'The Four Investigators' sounds even better than 'The Three Investigators.' Will you help Hannie and Nancy and me make a new sign? And new fliers?"

"Yup." David Michael was smiling. "Thanks, Karen."

"You're welcome. Come on. Let's go give Emily her Christmas tree."

Join the
Four Investigators Fun Force!

Super spy activities to try!

Okay, Detectives. You're now officially on the job. Your mission, should you decide to accept it, is to try these daring detective activities! Turn to pages 126–130 for answers to the puzzles if you get stuck.

Sweet and Sour Secrets!

All good detectives know how to keep a secret. Whether the message you need to send is sweet or sour, use this amazing disappearing ink trick!

You will need:
a lollipop stick
a saucer of lemon juice
ordinary notepaper

Here's what you do:
Dip the stick in the lemon juice. Using the stick as a pen, write your note on a piece of paper. Allow the note to dry. The message will completely disappear! Now pass the paper along to your fellow detective. Whisper to him or her that in order to read the secret message on the paper, the note must be held close to a light bulb. (Make sure never to touch the paper to the light bulb — you don't want to start a fire!)

The heat will make the message magically appear! But be sure your fellow detective can keep a secret, too. Once the note reappears, it is permanent.

The Amazing Alphabet Code!

This is an easy code to crack. It's based on the alphabet. In your code, each letter is represented by a different letter from the other end of the alphabet. Just use the code below to send your message.

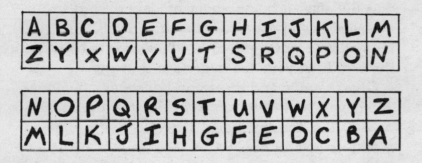

Now unscramble this one:

Kivggb hrnkov, sfs?

The Secret Decoder Code!

This simple decoder scheme will make sure your messages are only read by the right pair of eyes!

Here's what you do:
Copy the decoder on page 105, drawing A, onto two pieces of paper. Cut out the boxes. Put one decoder over a blank sheet of paper. Write your message in the spaces, as in drawing B. Now remove the decoder and write silly words in between the words in your message (see drawing C).

Give the note and the second decoder to a fellow detective. That detective will use the decoder to reveal your true message! It works every time — a perfect hole in one!

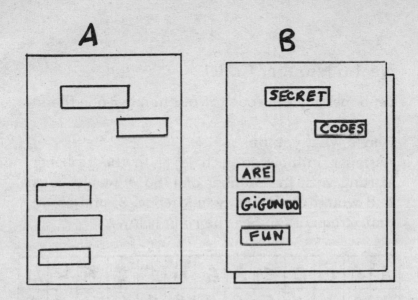

A

B

SECRET

CODES

ARE

GiGUNDO

FUN

C

THE SECRET WHISKERS
AND BLUE CODES
ARE WEARING
GiGUNDO UNDERWEAR
FUN

105

Neat-o Number Code!

Send messages in code to your number-one friend!

Here's what you do:
Assign a number to each letter in the alphabet, starting with the number one. So A would equal 1, B would equal 2, C would equal 3, and so on, until Z equals 26. See the code below.

A	B	C	D	E	F	G	H	I	J	K	L	M
1	2	3	4	5	6	7	8	9	10	11	12	13

N	O	P	Q	R	S	T	U	V	W	X	Y	Z
14	15	16	17	18	19	20	21	22	23	24	25	26

Then, write all your notes in numbers. Here's one for you to crack!

25-15-21 1-18-5 11-1-18-5-14'19 14-21-13-2-5-18
15-14-5 6-1-14!

Double Talking!

Nothing keeps a secret better than speaking in a language no one else understands. This is a simple secret language that can be spoken just between detectives! (Hint: It's still a good idea to whisper secrets. Be sure to use your indoor voice when you use this secret language.)

Here's what you do:

Divide any word into syllables. Drop the first consonant of the first syllable. Now say the first syllable. Then attach the consonant to the end of the word and add *ooba*. Do the same thing with the second syllable of the word.

Let's try one. The word is "secret." Eec*sooba* et*rooba*.

If the word is only one syllable and it starts with a vowel, just add *ooba* to it. That makes the word "I'm" I'm-*ooba*. For one-letter words, just add *ooba*. That's how "I" becomes I-*ooba*.

Now you're ready to try a sentence: Ou*yooba* are*ooba* a*ooba* reat*gooba* py*sooba*!

Hot on the Trail Puzzle!

Oh, no! First, Emily Junior was missing. Now, Boo-Boo, Karen's daddy's cat, has disappeared! But never fear — Karen, the great detective, is hot on Boo-Boo's trail. Follow the maze and help Karen reach Boo-Boo.

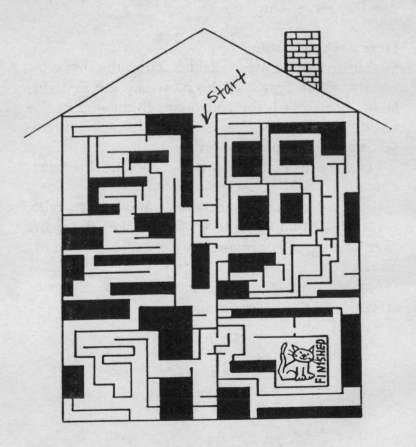

The Great Pie Mystery!

Someone has swiped a piece of Nannie's fresh-baked pie. Here are four pieces of pie. Help the Four Investigators figure out which piece fits the pie.

Something Is Wrong Here!

A good detective can always sense when something just isn't as it should be. The minute Karen steps into her backyard at the big house, she can tell something's wrong. Can you help her find the five things that are wrong with this picture?

A Candy-Coated Code Puzzle!

Here's a riddle. What kind of hearts are just like candy? To find the answer, fill in each blank with the first letter of the picture below it.

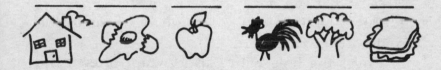

Make It Bigger

Every detective needs a magnifying glass to search for clues. Here's how Karen taught Hannie and Nancy to make their own magnifying glasses.

You will need:
a piece of cardboard
a medicine dropper
scissors
tape
water
clear plastic food wrap

Here's what you do:
1. Cut a hole about the size of a quarter in the center of the cardboard.
2. Cover the hole with plastic wrap. Stretch the wrap as smoothly as you can.
3. Tape the plastic wrap to the cardboard.
4. Lay a picture under the cardboard.
5. Put a drop of water on the plastic wrap.
6. Look at the picture through the plastic wrap and water. It's bigger than ever!

Laugh It Up!

Good detectives always catch the bad guys. These detective and criminal jokes are some of Karen's favorites, so you know they are gigundo funny! They'll make you laugh so hard, you'll have to catch something, too — your breath!

Q: Why are bakers like bank tellers?
A: They have their hands in the dough!

Q: What do you call a detective with a raincoat and webbed feet?
A: Duck Tracy!

Q: Why were the suspenders arrested?
A: For holding up pants!

Q: What happens when a detective takes a criminal's fingerprints?
A: They leave a bad impression!

Q: What happened when the detectives caught the hamburger?
A: They grilled it!

113

Those Amazing Animals!

Hide-and-Seek!

Karen sure had a tough time finding her poor rat, Emily Junior. Of course, she was kidnapped! But many animals *make* it tough to be found. That's their way of hiding themselves from their enemies. For protection, many animals have fur or feathers that blend into the background. The fur of some small animals turns white in the winter to blend in with the snow. White-tailed deer give birth to fawns that have white spots. That way, the baby deer will be able to hide in the snowy woods long before its legs are sturdy enough to run from danger! Many birds, like the pheasant, have feathers that are colored to help them blend in with their nesting areas.

Five pheasants are hiding in the picture on page 115. Can you find them all?

Gigundo-Fun Games!

Investigators, are you searching for something fun to do? Why not try one of these gigundo-fun games? They come highly recommended by Karen and her pals.

20 Questions (A game for two or more players)

You don't need a lot of kids to play this quickie quiz game. But as in any game, it's more fun with lots of people.

Here's how to play:
Say you are It. First think of a person, place, or thing. Then write your choice on a piece of paper and put it into your pocket. This will prove to everyone that you didn't change your mind half-way through the game.

Now the other players start asking questions. The object of the game is for them to ask just enough questions to be able to guess what person, place, or thing you have thought of. The other players can ask anything they want. The catch is, they can only ask questions that can be answered with a yes or no. The guessers are allowed to ask as many as 20 questions (that's where the name of the game comes from) before guessing. But the trick is to guess in as few questions as possible, because the person who gets the other players to ask the most questions before guessing is the winner!

I Spy (A game for two or more players)

This super spy game works a lot like 20 Questions. The difference is that the object you are thinking of has to be in the room you are in. Once you've picked an object, start the game with this short rhyme: "I spy with my little eye something ——— ." Fill in the blank with a word that describes the object you are thinking of. Then, just as in 20 Questions, the other players guess what you are thinking of by asking yes or no questions or by calling out objects in the room.

Here's an example:
Let's say you've picked an apple as your object. You'd say: "I spy with my little eye something *red*."
    Now your friends would ask questions like these:

"Is it round?"
"Is it bigger than a bread box?"
"Can you eat it?"

and so on, until they've guessed the object you are thinking of. There is no limit to the number of questions they can ask you. But as in 20 Questions, the person who gets the players to ask the most questions before guessing correctly is the winner!

Guess Who! (A game for four or more players)

This missing-persons game will test how good an investigator you are. You must use clues to find a mystery person.

Here's how to play:
Everyone gets paper and a pencil. Now each person must choose someone else in the room and write a short description of that person. When everyone is finished, one player collects the pieces of paper. That player gets to read each description out loud. It's up to everyone (except the person who wrote the description) to guess the identity of the person being described. And whoever gets the most correct guesses, wins!

Terrific Treasure Hunt (A game for eight or more players)

When you've got a gigundo-large group coming to your house, a treasure hunt is more fun than a million dollars! Any treasure hunt takes some time to set up. But your friends will think you have a heart of gold for doing it!

Here's what you do:
Before the group comes over, get out some paper and pencils. Now come up with a list of the "treasures" you want your friends to find. Items on your list can include easy things like a pencil or a piece of chewing gum, or they can include some really wacky things like flowered underwear and shower caps. Think of about ten items and copy the same list onto four pieces of paper.

When your pals come over, split them into four teams. Give each team a copy of your list and a paper bag to hold the treasures they find. (You might want to set boundaries for the hunt, too. For example, no one can leave your yard.) Now send the teams out. The first team to come back with everything on the list is the winning team!

The Four Investigators' Mystery Wordsearch!

Can you hunt down all of the detective words hidden in this wordsearch? The words go down, sideways, backwards, and diagonally.

```
A N O S T A W S D F G M
H A R D Y B O Y S N A Y
O N N D A R O D P I C S
L C L U E O S B M L R T
M Y I R B W O A B A I E
E D Z P R N L W X S M R
S R E S A C V N O W E Y
V E L V E K E K S D A Y
W W D A N S D R U M S C
```

Words to look for:
NANCY DREW, (Sherlock) HOLMES, (Dr.) WATSON, HARDY BOYS, CLUE, (Encyclopedia) BROWN, BOBBSEY (Twins), MYSTERY, CASE, SOLVE, CRIME

A Quickie Case to Solve!

Can you solve this Baby-sitters Little Sister quickie case?

Karen, Nancy, and Hannie are sitting on Karen's bed in her room at the big house. They are doing something secret. Karen is sure David Michael is peeking in her room through the keyhole, so she asks Nancy to turn off the lights in the room, to make it tougher for David Michael to see what the Three Musketeers are up to. Nancy walks clear across Karen's room to the light switch. She turns off the light and makes it all the way back to the bed before the room gets dark. How can Nancy do that?

Emily Junior, Where Are You?

Oh, no! Karen's rat is missing again! All these rats may look the same, but Karen knows which one is her beloved Emily Junior. The real Emily Junior is different from all the other rats. Which one is she?

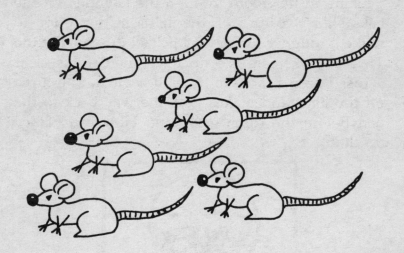

The Great Mystery Reading List!

Karen loves to read mysteries — almost as much as she loves solving them! Here are some of Karen's favorite mystery stories.

1. *TACK: Secret Service* by Nancy K. Robinson and Marvin Miller
2. *The Mystery in the Night Woods* by John Peterson
3. *The Boxcar Children: The Mystery of the Yellow House* by Gertrude Warner
4. *Encyclopedia Brown Sets the Pace* by Donald Sobol
5. *The Haunting of Grade Three* by Grace Maccarone
6. *Bunnicula* by James Howe

Let's Keep Track of the Animals!

Look down at the ground. You may just see some oddly shaped footprints in the snow. If the footprints were made by an animal, they are called animal tracks. Although you could probably follow the tracks long enough to find out where the animal went, it's not really a good idea. Most wild animals would much rather be left alone. So, instead of tracking wild animals, why not track down these tracks? On page 125 match the name of the animal to its tracks.

124

Rabbit

House Cat

Squirrel

Black Bear

Raccoon

Fox

Duck

Puzzle Answers

The Amazing Alphabet Code!

Answer: Pretty simple, huh?

Neat-o Number Code!

Answer: You are Karen's number one fan!

Double Talking!

Answer: You are a great spy!

Hot on the Trail Puzzle!

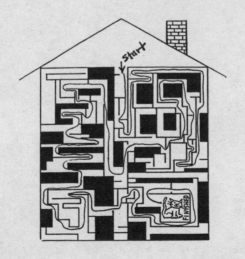

The Great Pie Mystery!

Something Is Wrong Here!

A Candy-Coated Code Puzzle!

S W E E T

H E A R T S

Those Amazing Animals!

The Four Investigators' Mystery Wordsearch!

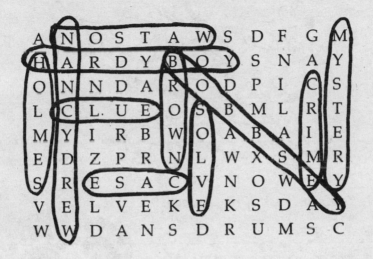

A Quickie Case to Solve!

Answer: It is still daylight outside, and some light is coming in through the window.

Emily Junior, Where Are You?

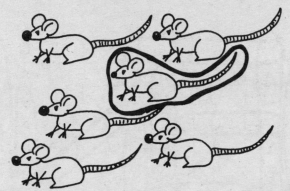

Let's Keep Track of the Animals!

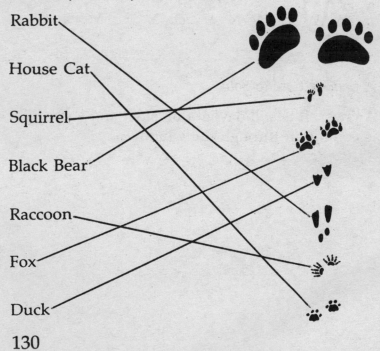

Rabbit

House Cat

Squirrel

Black Bear

Raccoon

Fox

Duck

About the Author

ANN M. MARTIN lives in New York City and loves animals, especially cats. She has two cats of her own, Mouse and Rosie.

Other books by Ann M. Martin that you might enjoy are *Stage Fright*; *Me and Katie (the Pest)*; and the books in *The Baby-sitters Club* series.

Ann likes ice cream and *I Love Lucy*. And she has her own little sister, whose name is Jane.

LITTLE APPLE ®

BABY-SITTERS

Little Sister ™

by Ann M. Martin, author of *The Baby-sitters Club*

This little sister has a lot of big ideas! But when Karen puts her plans into
action, they sometimes get all mixed up!

❏	MQ44300-3	#1	Karen's Witch	$2.75
❏	MQ44259-7	#2	Karen's Roller Skates	$2.75
❏	MQ44299-6	#3	Karen's Worst Day	$2.75
❏	MQ44264-3	#4	Karen's Kittycat Club	$2.75
❏	MQ44258-9	#5	Karen's School Picture	$2.75
❏	MQ44298-8	#6	Karen's Little Sister	$2.75
❏	MQ44257-0	#7	Karen's Birthday	$2.75
❏	MQ42670-2	#8	Karen's Haircut	$2.75
❏	MQ43652-X	#9	Karen's Sleepover	$2.75
❏	MQ43651-1	#10	Karen's Grandmothers	$2.50
❏	MQ43650-3	#11	Karen's Prize	$2.75
❏	MQ43649-X	#12	Karen's Ghost	$2.75
❏	MQ43648-1	#13	Karen's Surprise	$2.75
❏	MQ43646-5	#14	Karen's New Year	$2.75
❏	MQ43645-7	#15	Karen's in Love	$2.75
❏	MQ43644-9	#16	Karen's Goldfish	$2.75
❏	MQ43643-0	#17	Karen's Brothers	$2.75
❏	MQ43642-2	#18	Karen's Home-Run	$2.75
❏	MQ43641-4	#19	Karen's Good-Bye	$2.75
❏	MQ44823-4	#20	Karen's Carnival	$2.75
❏	MQ44824-2	#21	Karen's New Teacher	$2.75
❏	MQ44833-1	#22	Karen's Little Witch	$2.75
❏	MQ44832-3	#23	Karen's Doll	$2.75
❏	MQ44859-5	#2	Karen's School Trip	$2.75
❏	MQ44831-5	#25	Karen's Pen Pal	$2.75
❏	MQ43647-3		Karen's Wish Baby-sitters Little Sister	
			Super Special #1	$2.95
❏	MQ44834-0		Karen's Plane Trip Baby-sitters Little Sister	
			Super Special #2	$2.95
❏	MQ44834-0		Karen's Mystery Super Special #3	$2.95

Available wherever you buy books, or use this order form.

Scholastic Inc., P.O. Box 7502, 2931 E. McCarty Street, Jefferson City, MO 65102

Please send me the books I have checked above. I am enclosing $_____
(please add $2.00 to cover shipping and handling). Send check or money order - no cash
or C.O.Ds please.

Name_____

Address_____

City_____ State/Zip_____

Please allow four to six weeks for delivery. Offer good in U.S.A. only. Sorry, mail orders are not
available to residents to Canada. Prices subject to change.

BLS591

You Can Be the Lucky BIRTHDAY KID!

Join the

B·A·B·Y·S·I·T·T·E·R·S™

Little Sister

Birthday Club!

Happy Birthday to you! Join the **Baby-sitters Little Sister Birthday Club** and on your birthday, you'll receive a personalized card from Karen herself!

That's not all! Every month, a **BIRTHDAY KID OF THE MONTH** will be randomly chosen to **WIN** a complete set of *Baby-sitters Little Sister* books! The set's first book will be autographed by author Ann M. Martin!

Just fill in the coupon below. Offer expires March 31, 1992. Fill in the coupon below or write the information on a 3" x 5" piece of paper and mail to: BABY-SITTERS LITTLE SISTER BIRTHDAY CLUB, Scholastic Inc., 730 Broadway, P.O. Box 742, New York, New York 10003.

- -

Baby-sitters Little Sister Birthday Club

❑ *YES!* I want to join the BABY-SITTERS LITTLE SISTER BIRTHDAY CLUB!

My birthday is _____

Name _____ Age _____

Street _____

City _____ State _____ Zip _____

P.S. Please put your birthday on the outside of your envelope too! Thanks!

Where did you buy this *Baby-sitters Little Sister* book?

❑ Bookstore   ❑ Drugstore   ❑ Supermarket   ❑ Library
❑ Book Club   ❑ Book Fair   ❑ Other_____(specify)

Available in U.S. and Canada only.   BLS890

Kristy is Karen's older stepsister, and she and her friends are...

THE BABY-SITTERS CLUB®

by Ann M. Martin
author of *Baby-sitters Little Sister*

Don't miss these great books!

Available wherever you buy books, or use this order form.

Scholastic Inc., P.O. Box 7502, 2931 East McCarty Street, Jefferson City, MO 65102

Please send me the books I have checked above. I am enclosing $_____ (please add $2.00 to cover shipping and handling). Send check or money order — no cash or C.O.D.s please.

Name _____

Address_____

City_____ State/Zip _____

Please allow four to six weeks for delivery. Offer good in the U.S. only. Sorry, mail orders are not available to residents of Canada. Prices subject to change.

BSC591

KAREN'S SCAVENGER HUNT!

Solve the puzzle and you may win
FIVE of Karen's favorite things:

- **roller skates**
- **baseball hat**
- **flashlight**
- **backpack**
- **teddy bear**

25 Winners!

Karen's a detective, and now you can be, too! Some of her favorite stuff is hidden in the puzzle on the next page—find all ten items, circle them, and you may win **five** fabulous prizes! Just fill out the coupon below and send us **this whole page** by March 31, 1992.

Rules: Entries must be postmarked by March 31, 1992. Winners will be picked at random and notified by mail. Valid only in the U.S. and Canada. Void where prohibited. Taxes on prizes are the responsibility of the winners and their immediate families. Employees of Scholastic Inc., its agencies, affiliates, subsidiaries, and their immediate families are not eligible. For a complete list of winners, send a self-addressed stamped envelope to: Karen's Scavenger Hunt, Winners List, at the address provided below. Canadian residents send entries to: Iris Ferguson, Scholastic Inc., 123 Newkirk Road, Richmond Hill, Ontario, Canada L4C365.

No purchase necessary. To receive a copy of the puzzle/entry form, send a **self-addressed, stamped envelope** to **Karen's Scavenger Hunt Entry Form**, at the address provided below.

Fill in this coupon and mail the whole page to: **KAREN'S SCAVENGER HUNT,** Scholastic Inc., 730 Broadway, New York, NY 10003.

Name_____

Street _____

City_____ State/Zip_____

Age _____ Shoe Size _____

Where did you buy this *Baby-sitters Little Sister*™ book?
- ☐ Bookstore
- ☐ Supermarket
- ☐ Book Club
- ☐ Book Fair
- ☐ Drugstore
- ☐ Other_____ (specify)

BLS591

Can you find Karen's favorite things?

These items are hidden in the picture—circle all ten and you may win five prizes!

1. roller skate
2. backpack
3. knitting needle
4. toothbrush
5. broom
6. baseball hat
7. chocolate chip cookie
8. flashlight
9. teddy bear
10. rabbit's foot